Attention, Transformers fans!
Look for these items when you read
this book. Can you spot them all?

EARTH

STEREO

SPORTS CAR

Little, Brown and Company
Hachette Book Group
237 Park Avenue, New York, NY 10017
Visit our website at www.lb-kids.com

Little, Brown and Company is a division of Hachette Book Group, Inc.
The Little, Brown name and logo are trademarks of Hachette Book Group, Inc.

First edition: May 2011

ISBN 978-0-316-18628-5

10 9 8 7 6 5 4 3 2 1

CW

Printed in the U.S.A.

Licensed by:

TRANSFORMERS
DARK OF THE MOON

Optimus Prime's
Friends and Foes

Adapted by KATHARINE TURNER

Illustrated by GUIDO GUIDI

Based on the screenplay by EHREN KRUGER

LITTLE, BROWN AND COMPANY
New York Boston

Transformers are alien robots
from a planet called Cybertron.
They can change into machines,
such as cars and trucks.

Optimus Prime changes
into a big semitruck with a trailer.
Optimus Prime is an Autobot
who wants peace.

The Autobots have made
a new home on Earth.
They help their human friends
protect the planet.

Some Autobots came to Earth
with Optimus Prime many years ago.
Bumblebee, Ironhide,
and Ratchet are his friends.

Sam Witwicky was Optimus Prime's
first human friend.
Colonel Lennox is their friend, too.

Sam and Lennox help Optimus
and the Autobots battle
evil Transformers called Decepticons.

New Transformers have come to Earth
to join Optimus and the Autobots.
Wheeljack is one of them.
His vehicle mode is a dark blue car.

Wheeljack likes to invent things.
He made grapple gloves that fire hooks
to help Lennox and his soldiers
climb walls and large robots.

Mirage is a new Autobot, too.

He is one of the good guys.

He changes into a red sports car and likes to drive very fast. Mirage can appear to be invisible to confuse the bad guys.

The Wreckers work as a team.

The three Autobots

like to change into race cars.

The Wreckers are mechanics
who are helping a human named Epps
rebuild an Autobot spaceship.
They will make it fly again!

All of Optimus's friends mean a lot to him,
but one friend is very special.
This Autobot was found on the moon!

Sentinel Prime was the Autobots' leader
back on Cybertron.

He has a giant rust cannon
that can destroy metal objects.

Optimus is happy to have his friend back.
He shows Sentinel Prime
the Autobots' new home on Earth.

Some Transformers are bad guys.

They are called the Decepticons.

Their leader is Megatron.

He wants to take over Earth.

Optimus Prime and his friends
have battled the Decepticons before
and saved Earth.

Megatron never gives up.
He hides from the Autobots
in the sandy desert
while he plans his next attack.

There are new Decepticons
on Earth who will fight.
Shockwave is a smart robot
with a single glowing eye.

Shockwave rides a beast
that looks like a big drill.
They can tunnel underground
to attack Optimus Prime.

Laserbeak is another Decepticon.

He looks like a bird robot.

He can change into many forms.

Laserbeak can turn into a stereo,
a television, or a computer.
He hides in plain sight
to spy on humans.

More Decepticons hide on the moon,
waiting to come to Earth
and take over the planet.

Megatron gathers his army.
He transports the robots
from the moon to Earth
for a final battle.

Who is that helping Megatron?

It is Sentinel Prime!

He has betrayed the Autobots.

Sentinel wants to rule Earth, too.

Optimus Prime feels sad
that his old friend is his new foe.
But Optimus must protect his new home.
All his friends join the battle.

Sentinel aims his cannon at Optimus.
He says, "To save our own kind,
we must take over the planet.
I did not want to betray you."

A laser blast hits Sentinel's cannon,
giving Optimus a chance
to grab it out of the robot's hands.
"You betrayed yourself," says Optimus.

Optimus Prime's foes are defeated,
and his friends are safe.
Optimus has won this battle.
Earth is safe once more!